YAHOOTY Who?

An Illustrated Participa-Story

JMF Books

Published by JMF Books, LLC in California
Story and characters by Jen Oloo, Michael Rodriguez, and Ray Hodjat
Illustrated by Liran Szeiman

Copyright ©YahootyWho?™ 2017
All rights reserved

Dedications

~ Play ~

...as if you've only just met your best friend
and it's a Saturday with no responsibilities
...like you're in a magical land where fascination abounds
...because we can all play like children and search for Yahooties everyday

~ To Our Children ~

May you discover wondrous curiosities in everyday life
and know that you are never, never, ever alone.

A special thank you to Grandpa Walt
who saw Yahooties all around us and
to the dream makers
@kulaBrands.

When things get done around the house,
it isn't a fly, it isn't a mouse.

It isn't a monster, and isn't a bear
sneaking around in pink underwear.

If it isn't an octopus doing your chores,
then who could it be?

it´s YAHOOOTY

of course!

As he rushes along, he can't stop, he can't look,
and it's all cause of you when you opened this book.

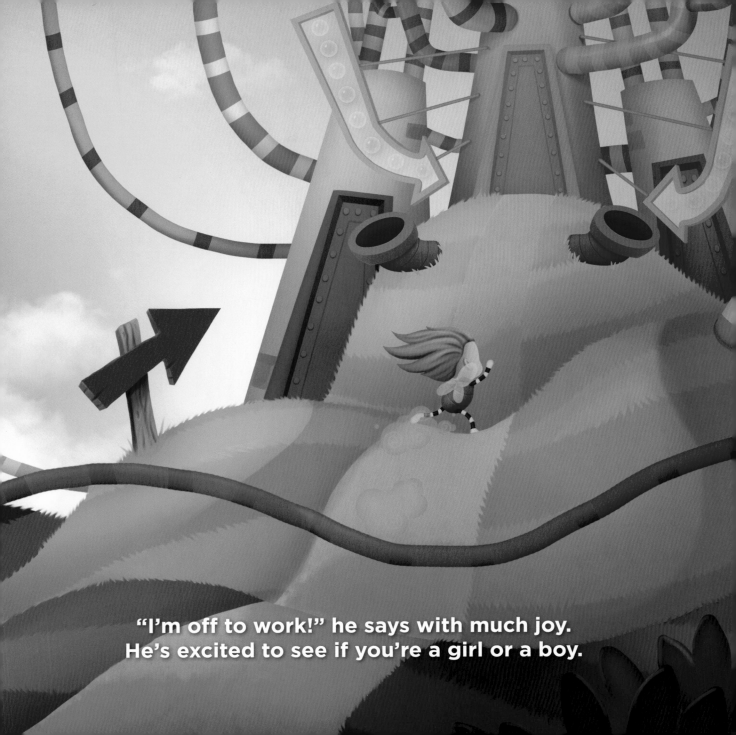

"I'm off to work!" he says with much joy.
He's excited to see if you're a girl or a boy.

Surfing through pipes, blue, yellow and pink
He arrives at your house, peeking out of the sink.

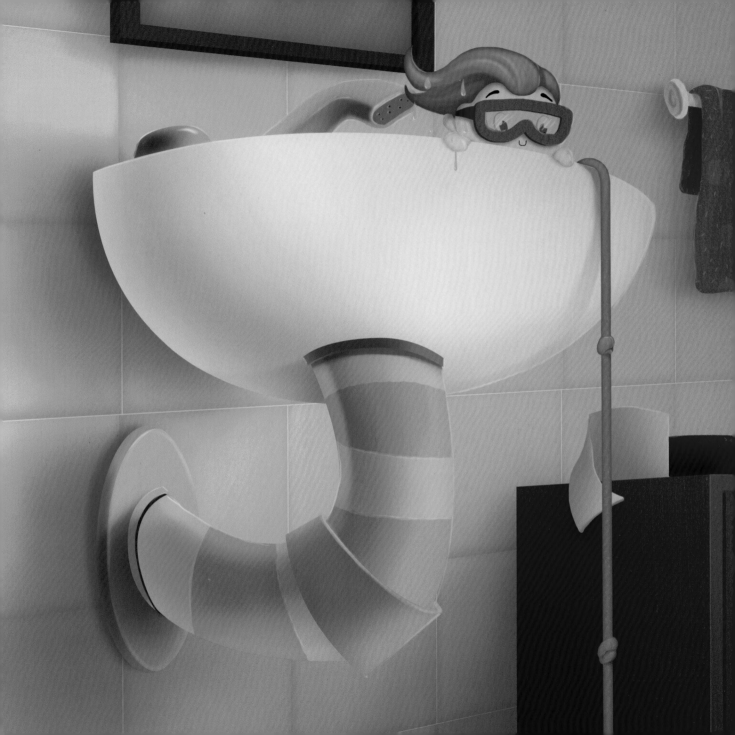

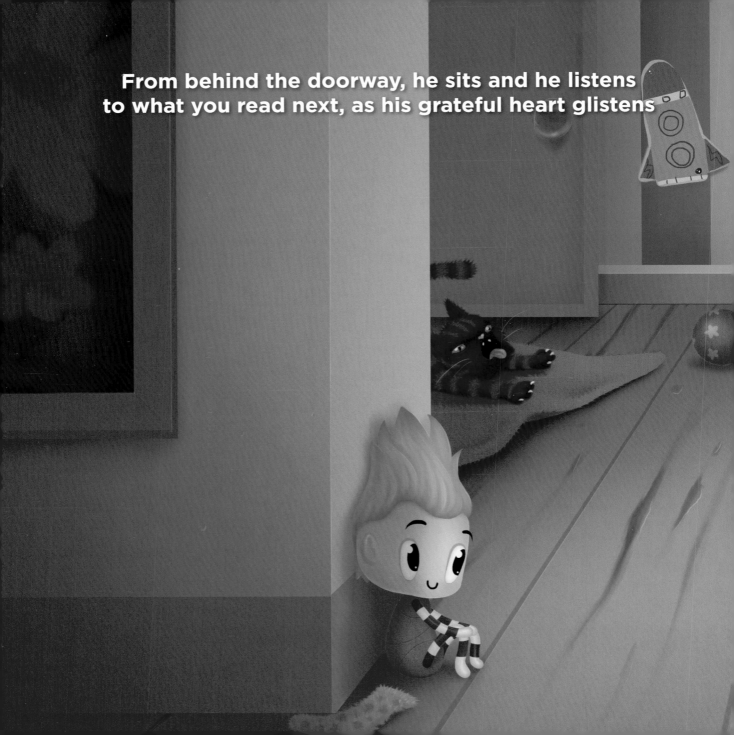

From behind the doorway, he sits and he listens
to what you read next, as his grateful heart glistens

In every house across the land,
lives a magical friend who lends a hand.

Leave him a sock and wait for a peek,
but he's far too fast for your eyes to seek.

Have you ever wondered, what keeps the water in for all you girls and boys, when you take a bubble bath with your favorite toys?

Who holds that drain tight? You say.

YAHOOTY does!
To keep your bubbles in, hooray!

Whooty-who you said did it?
YAHOOTY, I think...

...in return for a sock,
princess-purple and pink!

What about when you want your bread to be crispy?
I know only one person who would do a task so risky.

Who? You ask, heats up your bread in the toaster?

YAHOOTY does!
With his blazing toast-roaster!

Whooty-who you said did it?
YAHOOTY, that's right...

...in return for a sock,
extra-fluffy and white.

Planting is fun, but how do things grow?
With the help of a friend, who by now you should know.

Who? You ask, makes those plants sprout so tall?

YAHOOTY does!
In Spring, Summer, and Fall!

Whooty-who you said did it?
YAHOOTY, you know...

...in return for a sock,
filled with stars of yellow.

Have you ever gone to the fridge at night,
and a light appeared to put your food in sight?

Who turns on that light so quick?

YAHOOTY does!
Not some magical trick!

Whooty-who you said did it?
YAHOOTY, that's who...

...in return for a sock,
polka-dotted and blue.

My favorite YAHOOTY move that's so cool,
is watching the toilet twist like a whirl-pool.

Who makes my potty go downward bound?

YAHOOTY does!
With a sweet swooshing sound!

Whooty-who you said did it?
YAHOOTY, it seems...

...in return for a sock,
simply aquamarine.

You've tried to see him, and know he's about.
You sneaked and you peeked, but he's too fast, no doubt.

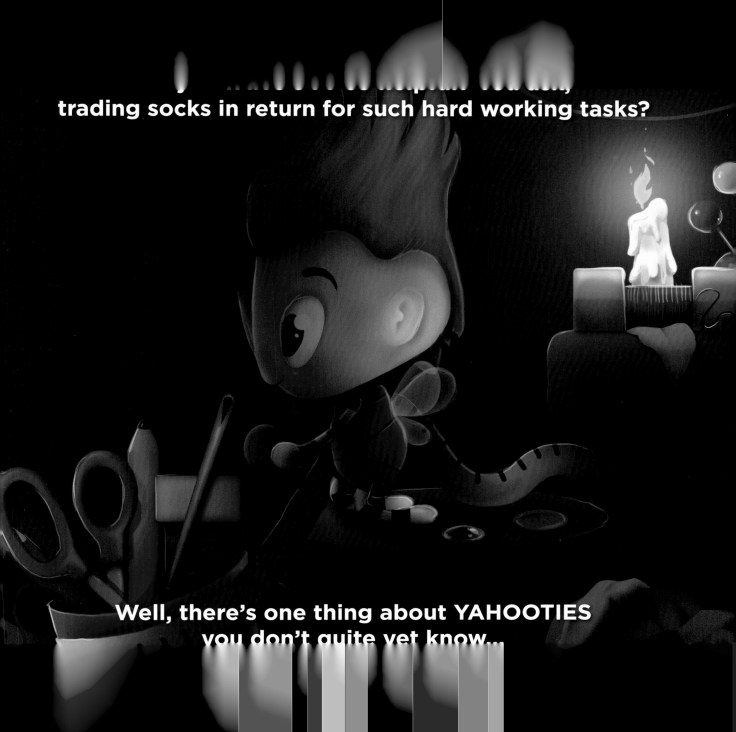

trading socks in return for such hard working tasks?

Well, there's one thing about YAHOOTIES
you don't quite yet know...

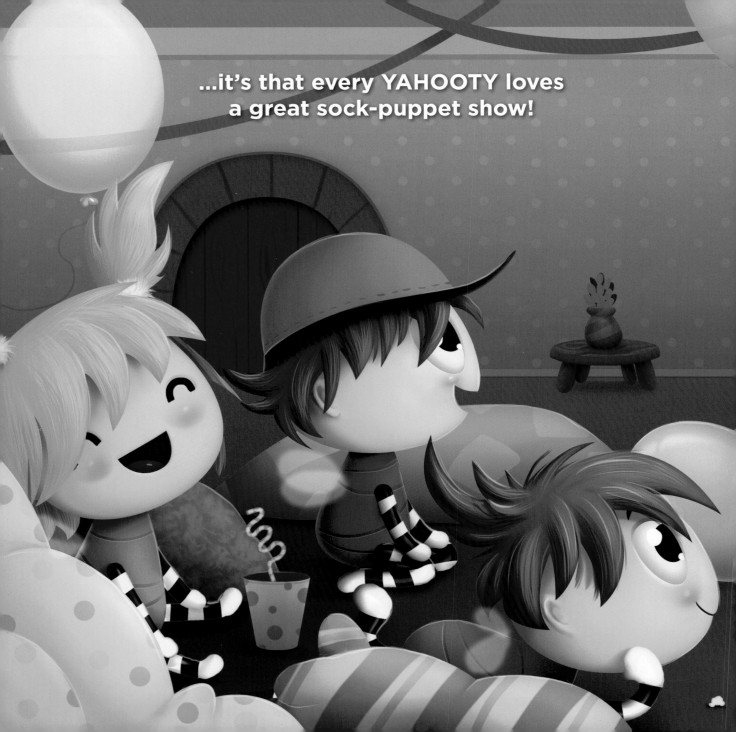

...it's that every YAHOOTY loves
a great sock-puppet show!

Now you know that
Yahooty loves sock puppets!
In fact, he has some special sock puppet
friends that would like to say hello!

HELLO!
MY NAME
IS FLUFF!

Join Us For More!

Yahooty Who?™ welcomes you to join our community online!
Download your FREE coloring sheets at http://www.yahootywho.com
and get access to extra special announcements, giveaways, and sock puppet videos!

Don't forget to follow Yahooty Who?™ on social media to share in the fun.
There are even opportunities for YOU to be featured in your own
sock puppet show creations!

**facebook.com/
yahootywho**

**instagram.com/
yahootywho**

**twitter.com/
yahootywho**